Rip Van Wi

Adapted by FREYA LITTLEDALE

from the story by Washington Irving

Illustrated by MICHAEL DOOLING

SCHOLASTIC INC.

New York   Toronto   London   Auckland   Sydney

ISBN 0-590-43113-7

Text copyright © 1991 by Freya Littledale
Illustrations copyright © 1991 by Michael Dooling
All rights reserved. Published by Scholastic Inc.

12 11 10 9 8 7 6 5 4 3 2 1   1 2 3 4 5 6/9

Printed in the U.S.A.   23

First Scholastic printing, November 1991

In memory of
my grandfather
F. L.

The Catskills are magical mountains
that change every hour of every day.
Sometimes their peaks seem covered
with golden crowns.
Sometimes they wear hoods of gray.
Always, they hold mystery.

At the foot of these mysterious mountains,
a colonial village once stood.
In the village, there was a kindly man
named Rip Van Winkle.
He lived on an old farm with his dog,
two children, and a scolding wife.

Morning, noon, and night,
her tongue was always going.
She would wave a ladle or broom
in his face and call him
careless, thoughtless, and lazy.

But Rip never said a word.
He just shrugged his shoulders,
rolled his eyes, and left the house
with his dog, Wolf.

Then his wife stood at the door
and shouted for all the world to hear,
"You're bringing ruin on this house!"

At the sound of her voice,
Wolf dragged his tail,
and Rip lowered his head.
But Rip kept on walking
until he reached the village inn
where he could be with his friends.

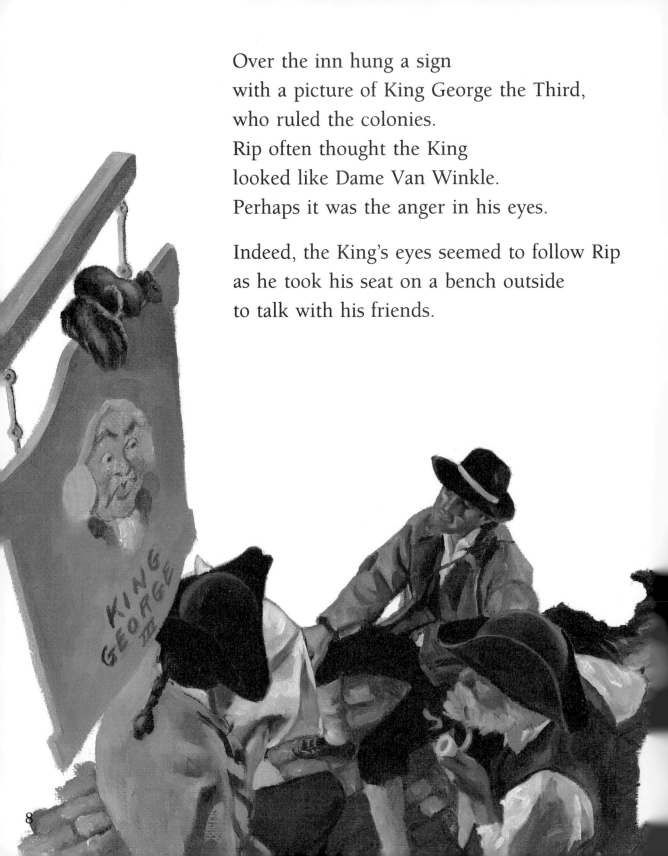

Over the inn hung a sign
with a picture of King George the Third,
who ruled the colonies.
Rip often thought the King
looked like Dame Van Winkle.
Perhaps it was the anger in his eyes.

Indeed, the King's eyes seemed to follow Rip
as he took his seat on a bench outside
to talk with his friends.

The schoolmaster, Derrick Van Brummel,
did most of the talking.
Brom Dutcher, the blacksmith,
knew all the village gossip.
But it was the landlord, Nicholas Vedder,
who was the most important man in the group.
Although he seldom spoke,
everyone knew what he thought
by the way he puffed on his pipe.
When he disliked what he heard,
he took short, quick, angry puffs.
But when he was pleased,
he puffed long and slowly.
Then he would look
at the picture of King George
as if he expected the King
to nod in agreement.

Rip spent many happy hours
in the company of these good men,
Wolf curled up at his feet.

Everyone in the village loved Rip —
especially the children.
He took them fishing,
built them a tree house,
and taught them to fly kites.
Sometimes he told them ghostly tales
about the magical Catskill Mountains
that rose over the village
like watchful giants.

Rip often helped his neighbors
milk their cows and pick their corn.
"It's no use working on my own farm," he said.
"Everything goes wrong.
My cows wander off,
my fences fall down,
and nothing grows but weeds."
And Rip was right.
His farm was wild.

His children were wild, too.
His son, Rip, was just like his father.
He only did what pleased him.
He even wore his father's trousers,
which he held up with one hand
like a fine lady holding her gown at a ball.
And his daughter, Judith,
put buttercups and daisies
in her long, tangled hair.

But Rip was not troubled
by his children or his farm.
His only trouble was Dame Van Winkle.

With each passing year,
her temper grew worse and worse.

She shrieked at Rip like an evil witch.
Her every word was a blow.
And wherever he went, she came after him.
His only escape was to go for walks
high up in the mountains with Wolf.
But he always returned home before dark.

One sunny morning, in early fall,
Dame Van Winkle threw a pail of water
all over Wolf.
The poor dog had done nothing wrong.

Wolf yelped and ran to his master
with his tail between his legs.
"Don't worry, my friend," Rip whispered.
"I'm here to stand by you.
Today we'll take a long, long walk."
And he gave Wolf a crust of bread
and rubbed him dry with a rag.
Then he sneaked out of the house
with his gun and his dog
and headed straight for the mountains.

Up, up, up he climbed,
higher than he'd ever gone before.
It was a wild and lonely place
where few human beings dared to go.
Tired and breathless, Rip stretched out
on the soft green moss that hugged the rocks.

Through an opening in the trees,
he saw the Hudson River far, far below.
Now and then a sailboat moved like a toy
along its shining waters.
For a long time Rip lay there in peace
with Wolf sleeping by his side.

The sun was low in the sky,
and the mountains cast
their giant shadows
over the valleys.
Rip knew it would be dark
before he could reach home.
What would his wife say?
He groaned at the thought.

Suddenly, he heard a voice call,
"Rip Van Winkle! Rip Van Winkle!"

Rip looked around,
but all he saw was a crow.
"Caaaw! Caaaw!" called the crow.

"My ears must be playing tricks
on me," Rip decided.
And he started for home.

The air turned cool,
and a sudden stillness
settled over the mountains.
Through that stillness
the same voice called again,
"Rip Van Winkle! Rip Van Winkle!"

Wolf gave a low growl,
and Rip felt chills
up and down his spine.
There, walking slowly toward him,
was a strange figure
with a thick gray beard.
Who is he? Rip wondered.
And how does he know my name?

As the stranger drew closer,
Rip was surprised to see a little old man
in old-fashioned Dutch clothes.
On his shoulders, he carried a large beer keg.
The little man didn't say a word.
He just made signs for Rip to help him.

Rip was frightened,
but he couldn't refuse.
So he and the silent stranger
took turns carrying the keg
up a rocky path.
Around them were gigantic rocks
and tall trees that broke the sky
into azure pieces.

From time to time, Rip heard
long rolling peals
like distant thunder.
"It's only thunder showers
somewhere in the mountains," he told himself.

At last they came to an opening in the rocks
where a group of strange little men
were playing a game of ninepins.
The men looked like figures
in an old Dutch painting.
All of them had beards
and were dressed in clothes
from long ago.

One had a big head and little piglet eyes.
Another had a nose as long as his face.
And one stout old gentleman,
whose skin was like cracked leather,
seemed to be the leader.

Rip thought it was very odd
that none of them smiled
or laughed or spoke,
even though they were playing a game.

Everything was quiet.
Only the noise of the rolling balls
echoed through the mountains
like rumbling thunder.

Rip's guide poured the beer into large flagons.
Then he made signs with his hands
for Rip to serve the men.

Trembling, Rip did as he was told.
The strange men drank in silence
and returned to their game.

Since they paid little attention to Rip,
he soon became less frightened.
When no one was looking, he even dared
to sneak a sip of beer
from one of the flagons.

Then one sip led to another
until Rip felt as if the ground
were spinning beneath his feet.
He sank down, closed his eyes,
and fell into a deep sleep.

Rip awoke on the very spot
where he had first seen
the little old man with the keg.
He rubbed his eyes and looked around.
It was a beautiful sunny morning.
Robins and bluebirds sang
from the treetops
while an eagle soared
in a cloudless sky.
"Surely, I haven't slept
here all night!" Rip exclaimed.

Then he remembered the strange men,
the ninepins, and the flagon.
"Oh, that wicked flagon!" he said to himself.
"What excuse can I give Dame Van Winkle?"

Rip looked for his gun.
But he only found a rusty old rifle
lying against a tree.
He whistled for his dog.
But Wolf was nowhere in sight.
"Wolf! Wolf! Wolf!" he shouted.
But Wolf did not come.

"Those men must have taken
my dog and my gun," Rip decided.
"I have to get them back."

As he rose to walk,
he felt painfully stiff.
"These mountain beds
aren't good for me," he said.

Rip spent the morning
searching for the men.
He was astonished to find
a mountain stream
bubbling down the rocky path.
Using the rusty rifle as a cane,
he had to make his way
through thorny bushes
along the sides of the stream.
Wild grapevines twisted themselves
like snakes from tree to tree.
Still, Rip moved on.

But it was hopeless.
He could find no trace
of the opening in the rocks,
or the strange little men
who had played ninepins there.
All he found was a wall of rocks
hidden by a dark forest
that seemed to hold secrets.

For the last time,
Rip whistled for his dog.
Only a flock of crows answered
from the leafless branch
of a dead tree.
"Caaaw! Caaaw! Caaaw!"

Poor Rip didn't know what to do.
He hated leaving his dog
and his gun behind.
And he dreaded seeing his wife.
But he had to go back home.
With every step,
he felt as if his heart were breaking.

As he entered the village,
he saw many people.
But he didn't know any of them —
not even the children.
Everyone stared at him
and stroked their chins.
After a while, he did the same.

Rip was astonished.
"How could my beard have grown
so much in one night?" he wondered.
Rip's beard was a foot long!

Everything was strange —
the people, their clothes, and the houses.
There were rows and rows of houses
he'd never seen before.
Strange names were over the doors.
Strange faces were at the windows.
"This can't be the same village
I left yesterday," Rip decided.
"I'm afraid the drink from that flagon
was a magic potion that addled
my brains."

Rip found his own house in ruins.
The roof had fallen in,
and the doors and windows were broken.
He called his children.
"Rip! Judith! Where are you?"
His only answer was the echo
of his own voice
through the empty rooms.

Rip hurried to the village inn
but it was gone.
Another stood in its place.
Rip thought he was bewitched.

He recognized the old sign,
but it wasn't King George
with a crown that he saw.
It was the face of a man
with a three-cornered hat.
Printed beneath were the words:
GENERAL WASHINGTON.
"Who can he be?" Rip wondered.

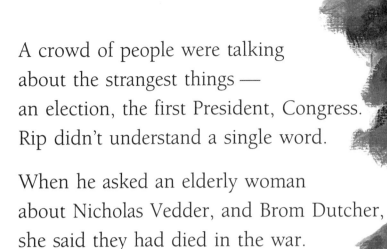

A crowd of people were talking
about the strangest things —
an election, the first President, Congress.
Rip didn't understand a single word.

When he asked an elderly woman
about Nicholas Vedder, and Brom Dutcher,
she said they had died in the war.

Had there been a war overnight?
That was impossible!

"What about Derrick Van Brummel?" Rip whispered.

"He fought in the war, too," said the woman.
"Now he's in Congress."

War! Congress!
What was she talking about?
Poor Rip was all mixed up,
and he'd never felt so alone.
"Doesn't anybody here know
Rip Van Winkle?" he cried
as the crowd gathered around him.

"Yes," said a man
with a booming voice.
"He's sitting on that bench."

The two Rips looked at each other,
but neither one said a word.
Old Rip couldn't believe his eyes.
It was like seeing himself in the mirror
before he'd climbed the Catskills.
"I must be dreaming," Rip mumbled.

"Who are you?" the man demanded.

"I thought I was me last night," said Rip.
"But if that's me on the bench,
I must be somebody else."
Everyone smiled and tapped their heads.

Just then, a young woman pushed
through the crowd.
She carried a baby in her arms.
When the baby began to cry,
she whispered, "Hush, Rip,
this old man won't hurt you."

Rip's heart skipped a beat.
"What's your name?" he asked.

"Judith Gardener," she told him.

"And your father's name?"

"Rip Van Winkle was his name," she said.
"He left home when I was a little girl
and no one has seen him since.
His dog, Wolf, came back alone.
I took care of Wolf
until he died of old age.
But I never knew what became of my poor father."

Rip had only one more question.
"Where is your mother?"

"Oh," said the young woman,
"one day she was screaming
at a New England peddler,
and she died in a fit of rage."

Rip let out a great sigh.
"I am your father," he told her,
"young Rip Van Winkle once —
old Rip Van Winkle now.
Doesn't anyone here know me?"

At that very moment,
the oldest and wisest man in the village
hobbled through the crowd.
Everyone waited to hear
what he would say.

The old man looked closely
at Rip's face.
"It *is* Rip Van Winkle!" he said at last.
"Welcome home! Where have you been
these past twenty years?"

"Twenty years!" cried Rip.
"Why, they felt like one night to me!"
Then he told his story,
and everyone was amazed
except the old man.

"Of course," said the old man.
"The Catskills have always
been haunted by strange beings.
Every twenty years, the Dutch explorer,
Henry Hudson, who first discovered the river,
comes back to the mountains
with his crew from the *Halfmoon*.
My own father saw them once,
playing their game of ninepins.
And I, myself, have heard the sound
of their rolling balls like distant thunder."

From that moment on, Rip was a free man.
He went to live with his son,
his daughter, and her gentle husband
in a snug little farmhouse.
And he did just as he pleased, whenever he pleased
without anyone scolding or nagging.

But it was a long time before Rip understood
that a Revolutionary War had taken place
while he slept in the Catskills.
The country was no longer ruled
by the King of England.
Now the country was free.
And Rip was a free citizen of the United States.

Still, the freedom that mattered
the most to Rip
was the freedom from his wife.
Whenever her name was mentioned,
he shrugged his shoulders,
rolled his eyes,
and whistled for joy.
She could never rule him again.

Rip told his amazing story so often,
everyone knew it by heart.
Some people didn't want to believe it.
But the old Dutch villagers knew it was true.

Even to this day, people tell the story
of Rip Van Winkle
and the magic drink in his flagon.
And when there's thunder in the Catskills,
they say that Henry Hudson and his crew
are playing their game of ninepins.